O9-AHW-354

To. Luke Hemkens.............................

.Happy. Halloween!. Love, Andrea.
Berumen, family ☺   Oct. 2016

This book invites you
to a Halloween Scare

Prepare If You Dare

A Halloween Scare in VERMONT

To my own little monster, Max, and his marvellous mum x

Visit the author's website! http://ericjames.co.uk

Written by Eric James
Illustrated by Marina Le Ray and Amerigo Pinelli
Designed by Sarah Allen

Copyright © Hometown World Ltd. 2015

Sourcebooks and the colophon are registered trademarks of Sourcebooks, Inc.
All rights reserved. No part of this book may be reproduced in any form or by any electronic or mechanical means including information storage and retrieval systems–
except in the case of brief quotations embodied in critical articles or reviews–without permission in writing from its publisher, Sourcebooks, Inc.

.

The characters and events portrayed in this book are fictitious or are used fictitiously. Any similarity to real persons, living or dead, is purely coincidental and not intended by the author.

Published by Sourcebooks Jabberwocky, an imprint of Sourcebooks, Inc.
P.O. Box 4410, Naperville, Illinois 60567-4410
(630) 961-3900
Fax: (630) 961-2168
www.jabberwockykids.com

Library of Congress Cataloging-in-Publication data is on file with the publisher.

Source of Production: Leo Paper Products, Guangdong Province, China
Date of Production: April 2015
Run Number: HTW_PO020215
Printed and bound in China
10 9 8 7 6 5 4 3 2 1

Prepare If You Dare

A Halloween Scare in VERMONT

Written by Eric James
Illustrated by Marina Le Ray

sourcebooks
jabberwocky

Prepare, if you dare,
for a big **Vermont** scare,
A tale of pure terror to whiten your hair,

A night full of sights that are best left unseen.
You ready? You sure?
This was my Halloween.

The werewolves
ho**wled loud**ly.
The moon shone so bright.
I stayed in my bedroom,
the curtains shut tight.

My heart started pounding,
my knees felt so weak,
But, being a brave kid,
I just **had** to peek.

I pulled back the curtains. My mouth opened wide.
An army of monsters had gathered outside!
They staggered and stumbled and lurched down the streets
With bags full of cookies and candy corn treats.

Emerging from sewers and houses and stores
Came creatures and critters with ravenous roars.
Then more came along from all over the state.
They filled up the streets at a dizzying rate!

From **Bennington**, **Barre**, and **Montpelier** too,
A mountain of monsters, the motliest crew,

All gathered together
for one **spooky** night,
To seek out the living
and give them a **fright.**

The thunder clapped loudly with terrible booms.
The witches dodged lightning and clung to their brooms.
The two-headed doggies tried chasing their tails,
And banshees let loose with their hideous wails.

The vampires hung out
on the street in their gangs,
And grinned, just to show off
their pearly white fangs.

The mummies moaned loudly and swayed side to side,
While Frankenstein stomped about town with his bride.

A lake monster spent the whole summer preparing
To go down to Vermont and do some good scaring,
But then she saw Champ—it was love at first sight!
They slipped off to cuddle and Kiss in the night.

A Sasquatch from Jay Peak State Forest appeared.
He thought he was scary and hoped to be feared.
But nobody screamed as he walked down the street.
Instead, they all laughed at his two dainty feet!

The creepies were crawly, the crazies were crazed,
The **Burlington** zombies had eyes that were glazed.
The ogres from **Rutland** were ugly as sin,
With big bulging noses and warts on their chin.

The ghouls danced around but were lacking in soul,
The gargoyles could rock, and the headless could roll!
Although the whole spectacle seemed to spell doom,
I foolishly thought I'd be safe in my room!

CALVIN COOLIDGE

But then something happened
that made my heart jump.
From somewhere below me
I heard a big THUMP!

I froze for a moment, as quiet as a mouse.
Yes, I could hear noises from INSIDE THE HOUSE!

I put on my slippers

and pulled on my robe.

I shook like a leaf

but I don't think it showed.

Then, slowly but surely,

I crept down the stairs,

Preparing myself for the
biggest of scares.

FLYNN CENTER

My hands trembled wildly.
I opened the door.
I still shudder now
at the horrors I saw.
The stereo spat out
some hideous sounds
As dozens of monsters
jumped madly around.

The sight was horrific. It made my skin crawl.
These monsters were having their
Halloween Ball!

And right in the middle, one monster loomed tall,
The **hairiest, scariest monster** of all...

He turned round and saw me.
I fell to my knees.
"I'm not very tasty,
so don't eat me, please!"

He beamed ear-to-ear
and broke free from the huddle,

Ran over,
and gave me a...

BIG

MONSTER

CUDDLE!

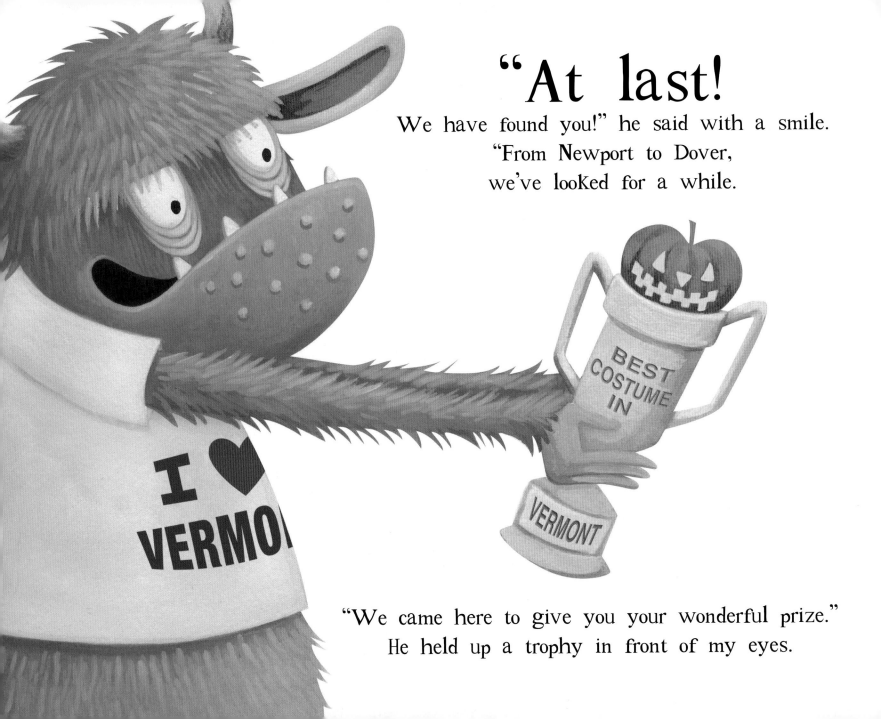

"At last!
We have found you!" he said with a smile.
"From Newport to Dover,
we've looked for a while.

"We came here to give you your wonderful prize."
He held up a trophy in front of my eyes.

"A prize? And for me?"
I replied with a grin.
"But what did I enter and how did I win?"
"You've won the first prize for the costume you're wearing!
It even scares me, and I'm tip-top at scaring!"

"This isn't a costume. I'm just dressed as me!"

"Exactly, the scariest thing you can be!

A small human child, with a cute button nose.

Your teeth are so shiny, you've only ten toes.

No hair on your face and no horns on your head.

The whites of your eyes are not glowing or red!

A bone-chilling costume! A horrible sight!

 A worthy ensemble
for Halloween night!"

We partied together
until the moon set,
A Halloween night
that I'll never forget.

And next year I won't
want to hide in my bed.
The monsters won't scare me,